KRISTA BENYUS

GRATITUDE ADJUSTMENT

AuthorHouse™
1663 Liberty Drive
Bloomington, IN 47403
www.authorhouse.com
Phone: 1 (800) 839-8640

Because of the dynamic nature of the Internet, any web addresses or links contained in this book may have changed
since publication and may no longer be valid. The views expressed in this work are solely those of the author and do
not necessarily reflect the views of the publisher, and the publisher hereby disclaims any responsibility for them.

Any people depicted in stock imagery provided by Getty Images are models,
and such images are being used for illustrative purposes only.
Certain stock imagery © Getty Images.

This book is printed on acid-free paper.

ISBN: 978-1-7283-3664-0 (sc)
ISBN: 978-1-7283-3666-4 (hc)
ISBN: 978-1-7283-3665-7 (e)

Library of Congress Control Number: 2019919655

Print information available on the last page.

Published by AuthorHouse 12/03/2019

authorHOUSE®

Mom – Thank you for being more of a mom in 12 years than most kids get in a lifetime. Your wisdom and example still guide me to this day.

Miss Mike – You always told me I should write a book...here you go!

Sally Ann Smiley was about to turn six, and as for any typical almost-six-year-old, life was simply stupendous.

But not for Sally Ann Smiley. She was anything but smiley. Sally Ann was a sulker. No matter what the day brought, no matter how fabulous, exciting, or wonderful, Sally Ann was a grouse, a grump, a grouch. She would brood, mope, and gripe. She was the epitome of gloom.

When Sally Ann's family went on vacation that summer, Sally Ann complained the entire time. Though she was almost six, she was much shorter than the rest of her family. "I can't see."

"What's happening?"

"I'm missing it all!" She complained often.

At the amusement park she griped, "I'm sick of riding the baby rides. I can't wait to be taller." Sally Ann could be heard muttering and mumbling, all while the rest of her family was having a ball.

At home it wasn't any better. Sally Ann had to share a bedroom with her big sister Jean, *a teenage big sister.* Jean loved to talk, text, and hang out with her friends, all the usual teenage stuff. "Jean never has time for me," Sally Ann would say, sulking.

School was more of the same—complain, complain, complain.
"I have to sit by Jordan, and he picks his nose all day. *Yuck!*"

"Mrs. McGuire never calls on me.
She likes all the other kids better."

"School lunch is never my favorite meatloaf-and-pickle sandwiches, and at recess no one wants to play with me," she'd report to her mom.

Sally Ann's mom knew something had to change. Sally Ann simply couldn't continue to be so grumpy, negative, and quite frankly ungrateful. So she hatched a plan.

Grandpa Ken was always Sally Ann's favorite. Mom invited him to visit for Sally Ann's super spectacular sixth birthday and to help adjust her ungrateful attitude. Sally Ann was thrilled to see Grandpa Ken. She loved him to pieces! Grandpa Ken always played with her. They'd have tea parties, play dress up, and perform plays in the living room. He even braved a night in her blanket fort.

While playing one day, Grandpa Ken asked Sally Ann why she'd been so ungrateful lately. Sally Ann gave her usual grumblings: "No one wants to play with me at school."

"I'm too short to do anything." On and on Sally Ann went.

"Sally Ann, I know you couldn't always *see* and do everything you wanted on your vacation this summer, but what *did* you get to see? What *did* you get to do?"

Sally Ann thought back. "I did *see* a cute bear cub sleeping high up in a tree."

"What else?" asked Grandpa Ken.

"I got to drive my own car on a racetrack. Oh, and I got to feed the ducks, and I got to pet the horses, and we even rode on a real train!" Sally Ann recalled.

"That's wonderful," Grandpa Ken said. "Did you tell Mom and Dad how much you enjoyed all of those things, or did you complain about the rides you couldn't go on?"

Sally Ann knew Grandpa Ken was right. She'd been complaining and focusing on all the stuff she didn't like instead of all the stuff she did like, and it was bringing everyone down.

"Sally Ann, it's very easy to complain, gripe, and grumble. If that's all we ever do, we become sad and bitter. Eventually people won't want to be around us. Can you blame them?"

Sally Ann put her head down. She knew Grandpa Ken had a point.

"We need to focus on the good stuff in our lives. We need to be grateful and appreciate all the good things we have and get to do."

"You mean like with Jean, I should focus on how she kisses me good night and reads me bedtime stories instead of complaining about how much time she spends on her phone?" Sally Ann asked.

"Exactly!" said Grandpa Ken. "Focus on the good stuff."

"And at school I should be grateful I get to sit near Trystan, my best friend, instead of complaining because I sit beside Jordan?" Sally Ann asked.

"You got it, kid," said Grandpa Ken.

"When we focus on the positives and are grateful, we stop seeing the negatives," Grandpa Ken said. "We're Smileys after all, and we need to stay that way. Smileys are grateful," Grandpa Ken said with a wink.

Sally Ann was grateful she had a grandpa who loved her enough to help her learn and grow. Sally Ann vowed to stay smiley!

CPSIA information can be obtained
at www.ICGtesting.com
Printed in the USA
LVHW070954030420
652017LV00004BA/95

TRINIDAD & TO

Images Coffee Table Book
BY MIA AYAANDEN

Made in United States
Orlando, FL
24 September 2024